Mama Grizzly Bear
Breezy Freezy Den Apts.
Too Chilly, Vermont XXOOX

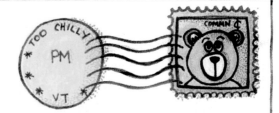

TOO CHILLY
PM
VT

The New Bear on the Block

937 Fuzzy Wuzzy Lane
Indamideluvda, Woods XOXXO

Written and Illustrated by
Staci J. Schwartz, MD

COMTEQ
PUBLISHING
MARGATE, NEW JERSEY

Published by:
   ComteQ Publishing
   A division of ComteQ Communications, LLC
   P.O. Box 3046
   Margate, New Jersey 08402
   609-487-9000 • Fax 609-822-4098
   Email: publisher@ComteQcom.com
   Website: www.ComteQpublishing.com

ISBN 0-9766889-2-1
Library of Congress Control Number: 2005936382

Illustrations by Staci J. Schwartz
Book & cover layout by Rob Huberman

Printed in the United States of America
10 9 8 7 6 5 4 3 2 1

For Marc & Jamie ☉
and in loving memory of D.A.S.

Once upon a time,
In an emerald-colored wood
Six houses in a clearing
Formed a charming neighborhood.

A kind and gentle creature
Lived snug inside each house:
A turtle, pig, a fuzzy duck,
A rabbit, squirrel, and mouse.

The neighbors lived in harmony
But then there came a day,
The squirrel moved out of town to take
A job with better pay.

Now, the empty house looked lonely
On the north side of the street.
The neighbors thought their neighborhood
Felt rather incomplete.

After many months had passed,
The house was finally sold
To a tiny grizzly bear
(For whom Vermont had been too **COLD**).

The neighbors had a meeting
To see what they could do
To make the bear feel welcome
In surroundings that were new.

When moving day arrived at last,
The duck prepared a cake.
She left it on the bear's front porch
Beside a garden rake.

The pig arranged a special lunch
With meats and sweets and more.
She tacked an invitation
To the grizzly bear's front door.

The mouse collected flowers,
And she tied them with a bow.
She left them in the mailbox
As a mouse-to-bear "hello!"

The rabbit hammered through the night.
He worked from dusk 'til dawn
To build a special birdhouse
For the grizzly bear's front lawn.

The turtle couldn't pick a gift...
A toaster? A cheese grater?
Perhaps he'd get to know the bear
And pick out something later.

The bear had found the house that matched
The picture on his dash!
He leaned out for a closer look,
And heard a sudden **CRASH!**

His glasses shattered on the ground!
(He *thought* that's where they were.)
He blinked, he stared, he rubbed his eyes...
His world – an instant **blur**!

"Oh dear..." he whispered to himself,
And settled in his seat,
"I cannot leave this great big truck
Stuck out here in the street."

The truck turned left, the truck turned right;
It creaked and squeaked and thumped!
The truck moved up, the truck moved back;
It rumbled, lurched, and BUMPED!

His tires bounced-up on the curb
KA-BOOM-A-BOOM-KAJING!
The mailbox snapped, the birdhouse crunched.
He could not <u>see</u> a thing!

He meant to push the brake to stop...
Instead, he pushed the gas.
The things inside the great big truck
Fell right out on the grass!

He stumbled slowly to the porch
And moaned, "For goodness sake!"
He saw no invitation...
His left foot squashed the cake!

He went inside to call a cab.
"Oh please! Take me to town!
If I don't get my glasses fixed
I'll knock my new house down!"

A beaver drove the taxicab.
He stopped and held the door.
"Get in my friend...a neighbor's near
Who owns an eyeglass store."

The beaver helped the little bear
And made sure he was steady.
"I'll take you home when you are through.
Just call me when you're ready."

The turtle said, "How do you do?"
The bear said, "Not so well...
I'm new in town and I've had grief
Because my glasses fell."

The bear then told his story;
What a **MESS** his house must be!
The turtle fixed the glasses
As he listened quietly.

Meanwhile, back at the bear's new house
The other neighbors stared!
What kind of **CARELESS SLOB** moved in?
They were nervous... they were scared!

"My birdhouse! **Smashed!**" the rabbit cried.
The mouse jumped up to see.
"He **squished** the flowers that I sent!
How mean can one bear be?"

The pig looked at her watch of gold.
The time said half past three.
"He never called or came for lunch.
What lack of courtesy!"

The duck was angry as she spoke,
"My cake, he stepped right in it!
A bear like this cannot live here...
Let's not waste one more minute!"

"The four of us have got to tell
The turtle what we know.
We *must* decide just what to do
To get this bear to **GO!**"

16

The turtle finished his repair.
The glasses looked brand new.
"There is no charge. Consider this
My welcome gift to you."

The bear said, "Thank you very much!
My glasses, fixed for **FREE**?
I'm grateful for your kindness
And your skill has helped me see!

The bear then phoned the beaver,
"Please pick me up once more."
The two drove off about the time
The neighbors reached the store.

Then, the neighbors told the turtle
Each detail (more or less)...
"This bear has ruined all our gifts!"
"His yard is such a **mess!**"

"He doesn't care about his things!"
"He's sloppy, rude, and mean!"
"And what about his *parking* skills?"
"The **worst** we've ever seen!"

"We do not want this bear around,"
The duck said with a frown.
"Let's send a message loud and clear...
Pack up and leave our town!"

"Just stop right there!" the turtle said,
"There must be some confusion...
You did not gather all the facts.
You **jumped** to this conclusion!"

"This bear is friendly and polite.
Delightful company!
He broke your gifts and trashed his lawn
Because he could not **see!**"

"His glasses needed to be fixed!"
Their eyes were open wide.
They never thought that this whole tale
Might have <u>another</u> side.

"To judge before you know someone
Is **NEVER EVER** fair!
You'll miss the chance to make good friends...
Like Mr. Grizzly Bear!"

"The turtle's right!" the rabbit said.
"We've made a big mistake.
Let's start again and meet this bear
And give his hand a shake."

The bear could not believe his eyes!
(The cab had reached his block.)
The beaver and the little bear
Stood on the curb in shock!

Pillows, clothing, lamps, and books
Were **not** where they should be.
Crates and boxes upside down...
Pajamas in a tree?!

He saw his mattress near a bush,
And as he looked around,
In the middle of the mess...
Tattered...**_gifts?_**...were on the ground!

Stems and petals from the mouse,
In pinks and blues and greens.

A birdhouse from the rabbit
Had been smashed to *smithereens!*

The invitation from the pig
Had fallen off the door.
The welcome cake the duck had baked
Was **crushed** upon the floor.

"What nice new neighbors," thought the bear,
"Who live on my new street.
The plans they made to greet me
Were so generous and sweet!"

His smile faded quickly,
Thinking how he might be viewed,
"If they don't know my glasses broke
They'll think I'm awfully **rude!**"

"I think I'll plan a party
With music, food, and fun
To show them I appreciate
The things that they have done."

The beaver said he'd *love* to help,
And scrambled to his feet.
"Your stuff is scattered everywhere!
Let's try to make it neat!"

They gathered his belongings,
And hung his clothes on racks.
Dishes, books, and pots were placed
Inside his den in stacks.

The beaver and the bear worked fast!
A busy, **dizzy** scene!
They never even stopped to rest
Until the lawn was clean.

The bear planned quickly for a feast
With yummy treats galore.
As he began to call his guests,
They knocked upon his door!

"How do you do?" the neighbors said.
The bear said, "Please come in.
I'd like to thank you for your gifts
And tell you where I've been.

My glasses broke when I arrived
So **blurry** were my eyes!
I know I've made a mess of things,
And I apologize."

"We know what happened," said the mouse.
"Poor Bear, what you've been through!
For all that we misunderstood,
We're really sorry, too."

The neighbors laughed, and ate, and talked
Until the break of day.
They even helped the bear unpack
And put his things away.

They took the time to *fully* meet
And grew to be great friends!
The neighborhood was now complete.
That's how this story ends.